DRAGON MASTERS

SEARCH FOR THE LIGHTNING DRAGON

BY

TRACEY WEST

ILLUSTRATED BY

DAMIEN JONES

BRANCHES™
SCHOLASTIC INC.

DRAGON MASTERS

Read All the Adventures

More books coming soon!

TABLE OF CONTENTS

THIS BOOK IS FOR MY PARENTS,

Tom and Carole Lubben.

Thanks, Mom and Dad, for raising a reader. — TW

Library of Congress Cataloging-in-Publication Data
Names: West, Tracey, 1965- author. Jones, Damien, illustrator. West, Tracey, 1965- Dragon Masters; 7.
Title: Search for the Lightning Dragon / by Tracey West; illustrated by Damien Jones.
Description: First edition. New York, NY: Branches/Scholastic Inc., 2017. Series: Dragon masters;
7 Summary: The Dragon Masters have two tasks: track down the newly hatched Lightning Dragon, and find his destined Dragon Master, a boy named Carlos, and convince him to trust them—but somebody else has dark plans for this particular powerful and wild dragon.
Identifiers: LCCN 2016035489 ISBN 9781338042887 (pbk.) ISBN 9781338042894 (hardcover)
Subjects: LCSH: Dragons—Juvenile fiction. Wizards—Juvenile fiction. Magic—Juvenile fiction. Adventure stories. CYAC: Dragons—Fiction. Wizards—Fiction. Magic—Fiction. Adventure and adventurers—Fiction. GSAFD: Adventure fiction. LCGFT: Action and adventure fiction.
Classification: LCC PZ7.W51937 Sbt 2017 DDC 813.54 [Fic]—dc23
LC record available at https://lccn.loc.gov/2016035489

ISBN : 978-93-8631395-9

First edition, March 2017
Illustrated by Damien Jones
Edited by Katie Carella
Book design by Jessica Meltzer
This reprint edition, August, 2024

Printed in India at Shivam Offset Press, New Delhi

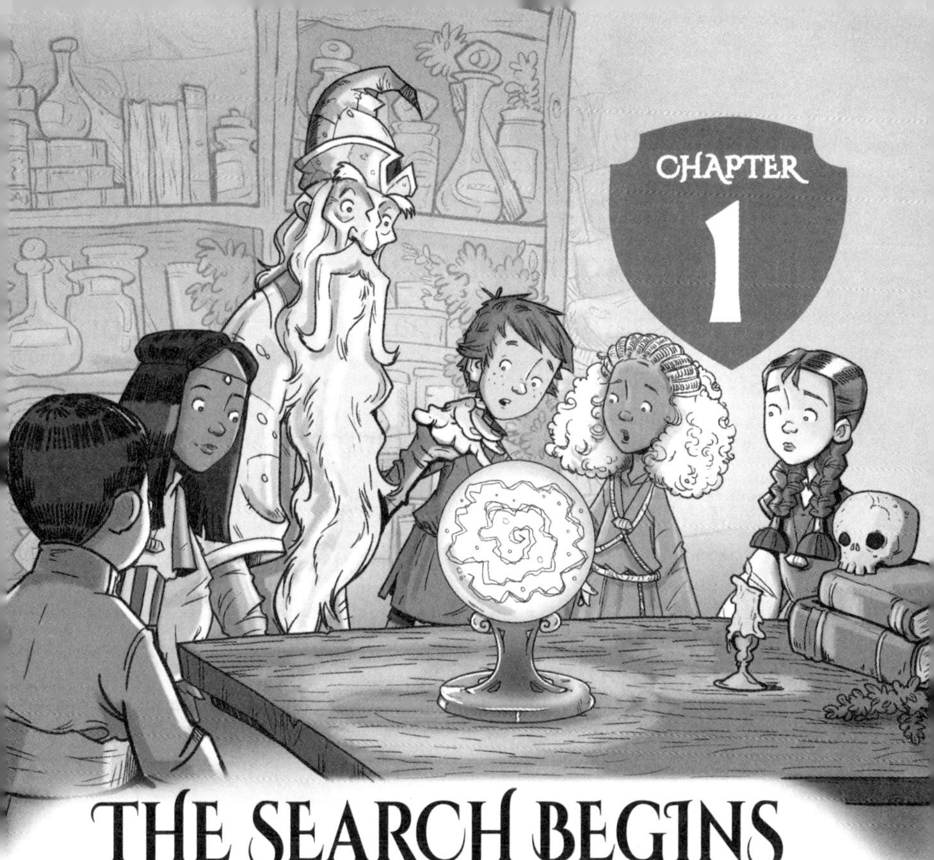

THE SEARCH BEGINS

"Do you see anything?" Drake asked the tall wizard next to him.

The wizard, Griffith, was staring into a gazing ball. Five Dragon Masters — Drake, Petra, Rori, Bo, and Ana — were watching the ball, too.

"No. The Lightning Dragon is flying quickly from place to place," Griffith replied. "He is hard to track down."

"Poor baby," said Ana. "He was just born yesterday!"

The day before, the Dragon Masters had found a crackling dragon egg in the Land of Pyramids. The baby Lightning Dragon had hatched in front of Drake's eyes. Then the dragon had flown away.

Now the Dragon Masters were back in the Kingdom of Bracken. They had gathered in Griffith's workshop to search for the dragon.

"That dragon is no poor baby," said Rori. "He can shoot powerful lightning bolts!"

"I think he was just scared," said Bo.

"He *must* be scared," Petra agreed. "He has no mom or dad dragon to take care of him."

Drake looked at Griffith. "What if we can't find him?"

Griffith looked up from his gazing ball. "Wizards all over the world are looking for this dragon in their gazing balls," he said. "One of us will find him soon."

"Can't we fly out on our dragons and look for him?" Rori asked.

Griffith shook his head. "The baby dragon could be anywhere. It is faster to use magic."

Ana looked thoughtful. "What happens when we find the Lightning Dragon?" she asked. "How will we communicate with him? He needs a Dragon Master, doesn't he?"

"Yes," Griffith replied. "But the Dragon Stone has not chosen one yet."

The Dragon Stone was a huge, magic stone that let dragons and their masters communicate with one another. Griffith had a large piece of the Dragon Stone in his workshop. Each of the Dragon Masters wore a small piece on a chain.

Poof! A cloud of smoke appeared next to Griffith. When the smoke cleared, a small, round wizard stood there.

"Diego! Do you have news?" Griffith asked.

"I do," Diego said. "The Lightning Dragon has been spotted!"

CHAPTER 2

CATCH THAT DRAGON!

Griffith waved his hand over his gazing ball. “I see him! He’s in the Land of Saxon.”

A scene appeared inside the ball. The baby dragon was flying over a village.

Lightning crackled on the dragon’s wings. Sparks flew from his body. The sparks hit a tree. The leaves burst into flame!

"Oh no!" cried Bo. "People are in danger!"

"The dragon looks scared," added Ana. "I don't think he wants to hurt anybody."

"But they might not know that," Petra pointed out. "Most people have never even seen a dragon before."

"Saxon is not far," Rori said. "We should go there right away."

"Worm could take us there," Drake said. Worm, his Earth Dragon, could do amazing things with the power of his mind.

Griffith turned to Diego. "You are a baby dragon expert. What do you think we should do?"

"Worm could take us to Saxon," Diego agreed. "But honestly, I am not sure what to do when we find this dragon. I know a lot about baby dragons, but I don't know much about Lightning Dragons – or how to catch them."

"Could we use a magic bubble?" Griffith asked.

"We could try," Diego replied. "But it might not be strong enough to hold him."

Griffith stroked his beard. "Hmm."

"Didn't one of your past students work with a Lightning Dragon?" Diego asked him.

Drake was surprised. "You had other students before us?"

"I did," Griffith replied. "I trained the very first Dragon Masters years ago. But Diego is mistaken. None of them ever worked with a Lightning Dragon."

"Where are those Dragon Masters now?" Petra asked.

Griffith's face clouded over. "That is not important."

Why didn't Griffith answer the question? Drake wondered.

"Come! What *is* important is that we go to Saxon and find this dragon," said Diego.

"Yes," Griffith said, clapping his hands. "Let's head to the Dragon Caves to make a plan!"

But just as they were about to leave, a bright green glow filled the workshop. Everyone stopped.

Griffith's Dragon Stone had come to life! Green light shot out of it.

CHAPTER

3

THE NEW DRAGON MASTER!

"What is happening?" Petra asked, as everyone rushed back to the glowing Dragon Stone.

"The stone has chosen a new Dragon Master," Griffith replied. "Watch."

Pictures appeared inside the beam of light from the stone.

"The pictures are moving!" Drake cried.

A boy and a white-haired woman were walking along a rocky shore. Ocean waves splashed behind them. Drake noticed that the boy had a white streak in his black hair.

Ana's dark eyes were wide. "We can hear them! It's like they're in the room with us."

The boy stopped and bent down. He pulled a net out of the ocean.

"Did we catch any fish, Carlos?" the woman asked.

"Just one, Abuela," the boy replied. "And it is very small."

"Ab-way-la?" Bo repeated the name Carlos had called the woman.

"That is the word for *grandmother* where I come from," Diego said. "And I know that rocky coast! They live in my kingdom, the Land of Aragon."

"Excellent!" said Griffith. "Then our new Dragon Master will not be hard to find."

"Does that mean this boy, Carlos, is the new Dragon Master?" Rori asked.

Griffith nodded. "Yes. The Dragon Stone has chosen him just in time!"

Drake stared at the boy in the pictures. He looked happy and peaceful. It reminded Drake of the day he had learned that he was a Dragon Master. He had been picking onions in his field when the king's guard had carried him away.

Carlos has no idea that we are about to come find him, Drake thought. *No idea that his life is about to change forever!*

THREE PLANS

"We must split up," said Griffith. "Ana and Bo, you will try to catch up to the Lightning Dragon. Rori and Petra, you will stay with me to research Lightning Dragons. And Diego, you should take Drake and Worm with you to fetch Carlos."

"Good thinking!" said Diego. "A friendly boy like Drake could help put Carlos at ease."

Griffith pulled a chain from a box. A small piece of the Dragon Stone dangled from it. He handed it to Drake.

"Give this to Carlos when you see him," Griffith said.

Drake looked at the stone. Holding on to it was an important job. "I won't lose it," he promised, tucking it into his pocket.

"Now let's head to the Dragon Caves," said Griffith. He hurried out of the workshop, and the others followed.

Griffith talked quickly as he walked. "Bo and Ana, you must keep track of the Lightning Dragon. When Drake and Diego find Carlos, they will find you. Then you can all try to bring the dragon here," he said.

Bo nodded. "Shu will put out any fires that the Lightning Dragon starts."

"And Kepri is very fast," said Ana. "She'll keep up with the baby dr—"

"Vulcan is faster!" Rori interrupted. She ran to the cave of her big, red Fire Dragon. "Why can't *we* chase after the Lightning Dragon?"

"Because you and Vulcan still need supervision," Griffith said.

Rori's cheeks turned red. She stroked Vulcan's nose through the bars of the cave.

"We don't need anyone watching over us. Do we, Vulcan?" she said. "We're fine on our own."

"That is dangerous thinking, Rori," said Griffith.

Drake wanted to ask why that was dangerous, but he was busy getting Worm. The brown dragon slid out of the cave. Worm had a long body, like a great big worm, and tiny wings.

Griffith turned to Bo and Ana. "Please saddle your dragons. Then bring them outside to the valley. I will meet you there shortly."

Bo ran to Shu, his blue Water Dragon. Ana raced to Kepri, her Sun Dragon. The white dragon greeted Ana by shooting a beam of sunlight from her mouth. The two Dragon Masters started putting saddles on their dragons.

Diego walked up to Worm's cave. "Are we ready, Drake?" he asked.

Drake's Dragon Stone started to glow.

Worm, can you take us to Diego's land? Drake asked in his mind.

He heard Worm's reply inside his head. *Yes.*

"We're ready," Drake said. He turned to his friends. "Good-bye, everybody, and good luck!"

Then he and Diego both touched the Earth Dragon. Worm started to glow with green light. The light flashed.

Whoosh!

Drake, Worm, and Diego were gone.

DIEGO'S MAGICAL COTTAGE

Drake blinked his eyes. He was not inside King Roland's castle anymore. He was standing on top of a hill with Diego and Worm.

The bottom of the hill sloped down to a beach of white sand. Beyond that, Drake saw blue water that stretched from the shore to the sky.

His eyes got wide. "Is that really the ocean?"

"Yes. Your first time, is it?" Diego asked. "Take a deep breath. Smell the air. There's nothing like it."

Drake did as he was told. The air smelled like salt and wind.

"It smells . . . clean," Drake said.

"It's good for the lungs!" Diego said. "Come, let's get you settled." Then he turned and shuffled up the hill.

Drake and Worm followed the wizard to a large cottage. It was made of bricks and wood, and had a mostly-straw roof.

This cottage wasn't like any Drake had ever seen. It wasn't one square room. This one was a rectangle. With another rectangle stuck to it. And another. And another.

This cottage is shaped like a big letter S, Drake thought.

Diego seemed to read his mind. "I had to add rooms onto my cottage. Too many books and potions," he said.

Then Diego looked at Worm. "Stay here while we get your room ready."

Worm nodded, and Drake followed Diego through the front door. The first room had a big fireplace. There were a few pieces of furniture around the room. Drake noticed a gazing ball on top of one table. Strings were draped around the room, on every wall.

"What are those white stones dangling from the strings?" Drake asked.

"They're called seashells," Diego explained. "Tiny ocean animals used to live in them."

Drake stared at the shells. He couldn't imagine what kind of creature would use one for a home.

Diego picked up a basket of mushrooms. Then he nodded to a bucket on the floor. "Let's go to the well and get some water for Worm."

They filled the bucket, and brought the water and the mushrooms to Worm. Worm gobbled them down.

"I'll make us some lunch, too," Diego said.

"Shouldn't we be looking for Carlos?" Drake asked.

"Ah, yes," said Diego. "You see, the coast is very big. It would take too long for us to search every village. But luckily, we have help."

Diego walked over to a window. He opened the shutters and whistled.

Drake watched, curious, as a bird flew up to the window. The bird had a white body and a black head. Drake had never seen a bird like it.

"It's a gull," Diego said. "I call him Bob."

Diego whispered to the bird. It squawked, and then flew away.

Drake's eyes were wide. "You can talk to birds?"

Diego nodded. "They're not all as smart as Bob, though. He will find Carlos for us."

Diego put bread and cheese on the table. Then he waved his hand over the gazing ball.

"Let's see if we can spy on Bo and Ana," Diego said.

Drake and Diego looked into the ball. An image appeared of Bo and Ana riding Kepri and Shu. They were flying across the sky – when suddenly, a yellow creature flew in front of them.

"They've found the baby dragon!" Drake cried.

CHAPTER 6

THE CHASE IS ON!

Drake and Diego watched the action inside the gazing ball.

The Lightning Dragon flew over a small village. The villagers looked up and pointed, their mouths open in surprise.

Ana and Kepri flew in front of the baby dragon. Bo and Shu flew behind him.

The Lightning Dragon flapped his wings. More sparks flew out. They rained onto the ground.

Ana was trying to talk to the baby dragon, but Drake couldn't hear what she was saying. Then Shu sprayed water droplets into the air above the dragon. Kepri aimed a beam of sunlight at the water.

A beautiful rainbow appeared. The baby dragon saw it. A calm look came across his face.

"The dragon doesn't seem so scared now," Drake remarked. "The rainbow is helping!"

"Maybe Ana can convince him to follow her," Diego said. "But that will be hard to do without Carlos . . ."

Ana tried talking to the dragon again. But then the rainbow faded. The Lightning Dragon flapped his wings. More sparks shot out.

These sparks landed onto the straw roof of a cottage. The straw burst into flame. The flame shot up, and almost hit Ana and Kepri!

"No!" Drake yelled.

Kepri dodged out of the way just in time. The baby dragon flew away! Shu quickly put out the flames. Then Bo and Ana raced after the speeding dragon.

The gazing ball went dark.

THE RATTLING SHELLS

"How will Bo and Ana ever catch that dragon?" Drake asked.

Diego nodded. "I am afraid that only his Dragon Master will be able to calm him. I hope Bob finds Carlos soon."

"Isn't there anything else we can do?" Drake asked.

Diego shook his head. "We must wait. Bob has never failed me."

Drake frowned. It felt wrong to be sitting around, when Bo and Ana were flying after a dragon that shot sparks.

"Come," Diego said. "Let's eat and then get Worm's room ready for tonight."

Diego led Drake through the twisting cottage. Drake saw that strings of seashells hung on every wall. They passed a room full of plants. Another room held jars and bottles filled with colorful liquids. Another room was full of books.

They finally came to the last room, which looked almost like a stable. There was hay on the floor. Two big doors opened up to the outside. This room had strings of seashells on the walls, too.

"I built this room in case any of Griffith's dragons came to visit me," Diego explained. "Worm is my first guest!"

Diego and Drake swept out the stable.

When they finished, they opened the doors. Worm slid inside and curled up in the hay, smiling.

Drake turned to Diego. "What were those other rooms we passed through?"

"Ah, I shall give you a tour!" he said. "Follow me."

Diego led Drake back through the cottage. In the first room, the wizard showed Drake books about baby dragons.

In the second room, Diego mixed a red potion and a blue potion together in a glass. There was a puff of smoke – and a purple stone shaped like an onion appeared.

"A reminder of home," Diego said, giving it to Drake.

"Thanks!" said Drake.

In the third room, Diego handed Drake a dried green plant.

"This one is good for keeping away bad energy," he said. "It's also very tasty in stew. Which reminds me, we should get dinner started."

They went to the kitchen, where Diego gave Drake some carrots to chop. As Drake picked up a carrot, he heard a rattling noise. He looked up. The strings were shaking and the shells were clinking!

Diego quickly took his wand out of his pocket.

"Why are the shells moving?" Drake asked.

Diego didn't answer. He waved the wand and muttered some strange words. A blue light streamed from the wand and snaked through the cottage.

When the light faded, Diego ran outside. He looked up at the sky.

"What just happened?" Drake asked.

"The shells work like a magical alarm," Diego said. "They rattle when danger is near."

Drake shivered. "Danger?" he asked.

"Robbers, magical creatures, dark wizards, things like that," Diego replied. "But whoever it was, they're gone now. The blue light from my wand chased them away."

Diego didn't say anything more about the shells. He and Drake made a stew and cooked it over the fire. When it got dark, Diego closed the shutters. He brought out a straw mattress for Drake, along with a blanket and a pillow. Then he set them next to the fire.

"It gets chilly at night," Diego said. "You'll be warm here."

"Thank you," Drake said, and he climbed under the blanket.

The room was dark, but he could see the white gleam of the seashells, just before he closed his eyes.

THE SEARCH CONTINUES

The next morning, Diego and Drake were up with the sun. There was still no sign of Bob.

"Let's pop back to the castle," said Diego. "Perhaps the others have learned something that can help us. Worm can stay here and keep watch."

"I'll tell Worm," Drake said. Then he ran to the stable.

"Keep an eye on things, please," Drake told his dragon. "If the shells rattle again, let me know."

Worm nodded as Diego walked over, holding his wand. "Ready?" he asked. "Stand close!"

Drake obeyed.

"Will your magic feel the same as when Worm transports us?" Drake asked.

"Just about," Diego answered. Then he waved his wand.

Drake started to feel tingly. Then, before he knew it . . .

Poof! They were back inside Griffith's workshop. Petra and Rori were sitting at a table. The table was piled with books. Rori was yawning. Griffith was standing next to them.

"Good morning!" Griffith said. "Do you have news?"

"We haven't found Carlos yet," Diego replied. "Have you three learned anything useful about Lightning Dragons?"

"We learned that Lightning Dragons are not easy to catch," Griffith replied.

"I could've told you that without reading twenty books," Rori pointed out.

Griffith frowned at Rori.

"We also found out that they like to eat sugar, or anything sweet," Petra said. "And one book says they'll calm down if you can find a way to drain their energy."

"But the book didn't say *how* to drain their energy," Rori added.

Griffith sighed. "I'm afraid Rori's right. We still have much to learn."

"Keep at it! I am sure you'll find out more soon," Diego said. "Before we go, Griffith, I must speak with you."

The two wizards stepped aside and spoke in whispers. Drake knew that Diego was telling Griffith about the shaking seashells.

When the wizards finished, Drake said good-bye to his friends.

Then Diego and Drake *poofed* back to the cottage.

When they walked inside, Bob was sitting on the kitchen table.

"Bob!" Diego said. The bird hopped onto Diego's shoulder and started chattering.

"Very good, Bob. Thank you," Diego said.

The bird flew away and Diego turned to Drake. "Looks like we're off again!"

"Did he find Carlos?" Diego asked.

"He did!" Diego replied. He waved his wand. A second later, they were standing in front of a cottage in a busy fishing village. Drake could see boats floating in the ocean. Men carrying buckets and nets walked down to the water. A boy with a white streak in his black hair was staring at Drake and Diego.

"Where did you two come from?" the boy asked.

"Hello, Carlos," Diego said. "I am Diego, and this is my friend, Drake."

Carlos's dark eyes narrowed. "How did you know my name?"

"I am a wizard," Diego explained. "We have come to find you."

"You're a Dragon Master!" Drake blurted out. He was excited to tell Carlos the news.

"A dragon what?" Carlos asked, frowning.

Then the cottage door opened. A white-haired woman stepped out.

"Carlos, who are you speaking to?" she asked. Then she spotted Diego and her eyes grew wide. "What are you waiting for? Invite this wizard and his friend inside!"

Carlos nodded. "Yes, Abuela," he said.

He waved at Diego and Drake to follow him. Drake noticed that Carlos was still frowning.

He doesn't trust us yet, Drake thought, and that worried him. The Lightning Dragon was too hard to catch without his Dragon Master. *I hope we can make him believe us!*

DRAGONS AREN'T REAL!

"Come, have a seat," Carlos's grandmother said. "I am Nita, and this is my grandson, Carlos."

She shuffled to a rickety table in the center of the one-room cottage. Drake, Diego, and Carlos followed her and sat down. Drake noticed there wasn't much other furniture except for two straw beds. But the room was scrubbed clean.

"Please tell me, why has a wizard come to our simple cottage?" Nita asked. Her dark eyes gleamed with excitement as she looked at Diego.

"He is not a wizard, Abuela, he is a storyteller," Carlos interrupted. "These two were talking about dragons."

"We do have a story to tell you, young man," Diego said, leaning forward. "But it is a true story. A new dragon hatched a few days ago. A Lightning Dragon. And the Dragon Stone has chosen *you* to be his master."

Carlos shook his head. "Dragons aren't real."

Diego looked at Drake. "Show him the stone."

Drake took the piece of the Dragon Stone from his pocket and held it out to Carlos. "See? It's like mine. I was chosen, too – just like you. My Dragon Stone helps me connect with my dragon."

"If you have a dragon, then where is he?" Carlos asked.

"Come with us, and we can show you," Diego said.

Carlos folded his arms. "Are you kidding? I'm not going anywhere with you two."

Drake looked at Diego. "I have an idea," he said. Drake closed his eyes. He touched his Dragon Stone. He wasn't sure if he could contact Worm from so far away.

Then the stone began to glow.

Worm, can you hear me? Drake asked, in his mind. *If you can, please find me. I am at Carlos's cottage by the sea. I'll be outside, in the back.*

To his surprise, Worm replied right away.

I will find you.

Drake opened his eyes. "Come outside."

Carlos didn't move, but his grandmother poked his arm. "Go, Carlos."

With a sigh, he stepped outside with Drake and Diego. A cloud of light was shimmering behind the cottage.

Then Worm appeared!

Drake looked at Carlos. The boy's mouth was wide open.

"It's a trick," Carlos said.

Drake walked to Worm and hugged his neck. "No, it's not. He's real. And he's friendly. Come see."

Carlos slowly walked up to Worm, his eyes wide. He put a hand on Worm's neck.

"So many scales," he whispered to himself.

After a minute, Carlos turned to Diego.

"This is all real, isn't it?" he said. "You're a real wizard. And this is a real dragon."

"As real as rain!" Diego said.

Drake smiled. He held out the Dragon Stone again. This time, Carlos took it. He put the chain around his neck.

"So what does it mean, to be a Dragon Master?" Carlos asked.

"You will need to come with us to the Kingdom of Bracken," Diego replied. "You will live at the castle and learn how to work with your dragon."

Carlos looked back at the cottage. "My grandmother is my only family. Who will fetch the water for her? And bring wood for the fire? I'm sorry, but I can't leave her."

Drake knew how Carlos felt. It had not been easy to leave his mother. But at least he knew his brothers would take care of her.

Drake couldn't tell Carlos to leave his grandmother. It just didn't feel right.

But how will we catch the Lightning Dragon without him? Drake wondered.

Suddenly, there was a loud *boom!* Drake looked to the sky. Gray clouds were quickly moving in. Rain started to shower down.

"The boats!" Carlos cried. "I must help the fishermen!"

Then he ran toward the sea.

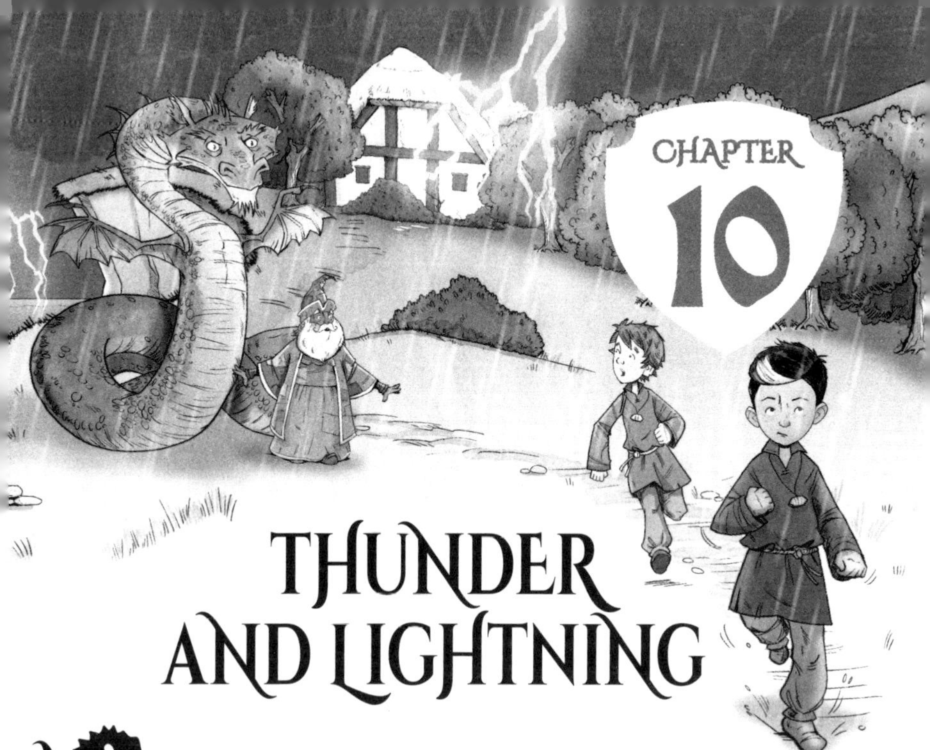

CHAPTER 10

THUNDER AND LIGHTNING

Crackle! A lightning bolt flashed.

Boom! Thunder shook the sky.

"This is a dangerous storm!" Diego yelled. "Get inside, Drake!"

"We have to help Carlos!" Drake yelled back. Then he turned to his dragon. "Worm, stay here so you don't scare the villagers."

Drake ran after Carlos. Shaking his head, Diego followed them.

Drake and Diego caught up to Carlos, who was helping a fisherman get safely back to shore. Drake and the fisherman pushed the boat. Carlos and Diego pulled on ropes. They got the boat onto the sand.

Boom! Crackle! Another lightning bolt flashed. It raced toward the ground near Drake.

"Watch out!" Carlos said, pulling Drake out of the way.

The lightning bolt hit the sandy ground a few feet away. Drake watched as the bolt seemed to disappear into the earth.

"That was close!" Drake said. "Thanks, Carlos."

Carlos ran to help another fisherman. As he did, the clouds floated away. The rain stopped. The sky turned blue once more.

"That was a very strange storm," Diego remarked, frowning.

Then the fishermen all stopped what they were doing. Their mouths dropped open and their eyes were wide.

Drake turned and saw Worm slithering toward the shore.

"Worm!" Drake called out. *Why is Worm here? I had told him to stay out of sight.*

Then he heard a noise.

Crackle! Crackle!

Is the storm back? Drake wondered, looking up.

The Lightning Dragon swooped down from the sky!

CHAPTER 11

YOU CAN'T CATCH LIGHTNING!

Kepri flew right behind the Lightning Dragon, with Ana on her back. Bo and Shu were close behind.

The Lightning Dragon hovered in the air, flapping his wings. Sparks shot from his body.

The frightened fishermen all ran away, leaving Diego, Drake, Worm, and Carlos alone on the shore.

“That dragon is like a living lightning storm!” Carlos said.

“He is a baby Lightning Dragon,” Drake explained. “And you’re his Dragon Master.”

“He must’ve flown here because you put on your Dragon Stone, Carlos,” said Diego.

“He could fly away any minute!” Ana called down from Kepri. “He moves fast!”

“We must catch him!” Diego cried.

“How?” Carlos asked. “You can’t catch lightning!”

"Ah, but he is a Lightning *Dragon*, and you are his master," said Diego. "You must find a way to calm him. I will try something in the meantime . . ."

Diego held out his wizard's wand. Blue light sparked from the end. Carlos gasped. More blue light flowed out of the wand, forming a big bubble.

Drake had seen Diego make a magic bubble once before. He and Griffith had used it to capture an evil wizard named Maldred.

The bubble floated up and surrounded the baby Lightning Dragon. He let out a high-pitched cry.

Eeeeeeeeeeeeee!

The baby dragon thrashed his wings. Small lightning bolts flashed from his body.

Pop! The bubble burst.

The dragon flew in wild circles above the beach.

"Ow!" Carlos yelled.

"What's wrong?" Drake asked, running over to him.

Carlos had his hands over his ears. His Dragon Stone was glowing bright green.

"I can hear sounds in my head!" he cried. "Like someone is crying out for help!"

"That is your dragon," Drake said. "You're making a connection!"

“Good for you, Carlos!” Diego cheered. “Now talk to him. In your mind. Try to calm him down.”

Carlos closed his eyes. He made a face like he was thinking very hard.

The Lightning Dragon started hovering again. But more lightning bolts shot out every time he flapped his wings.

“I can try another magic bubble,” Diego said. “But I don’t know if it will hold him.”

Drake remembered something. “Petra said the dragon would calm down if we found a way to drain its energy. Is there some way we can do that?”

Then Drake heard Worm’s voice in his head.

I am earth.

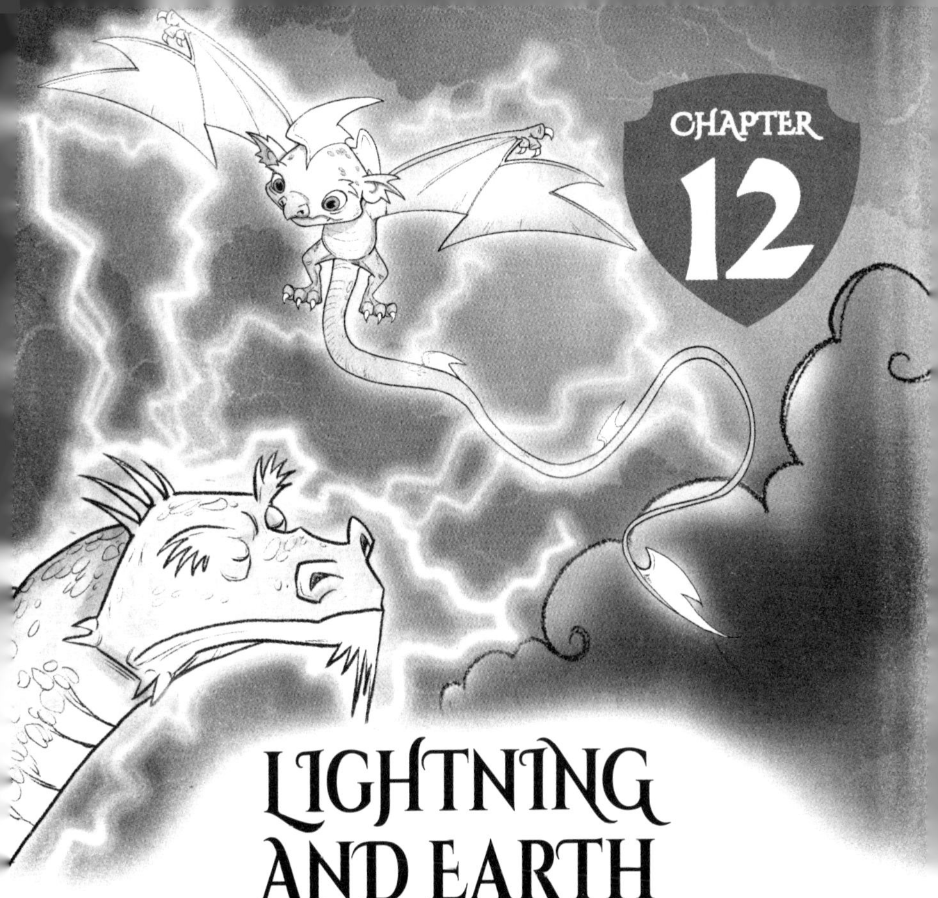

CHAPTER 12

LIGHTNING AND EARTH

Worm raced toward the baby Lightning Dragon. He stopped underneath the dragon. He closed his eyes as he let the lightning bolts zap him.

"Worm!" Ana yelled. She and Bo quickly flew down toward the beach.

But Drake wasn't worried. He knew what Worm was doing. The lightning bolts didn't shock Worm. When they hit him, Worm's body absorbed them.

Just like the ground had absorbed the lightning that hit the beach! Drake thought. *Worm is an Earth Dragon, so he can drain the Lightning Dragon's energy!*

Kepri and Shu landed on the shore. Ana and Bo climbed off and ran over to Drake.

"Don't worry about Worm," Drake said. "Look!"

A line of energy flowed between the Lightning Dragon and Worm. The baby dragon's wings started to flap more slowly. He stopped shooting sparks.

Diego was almost ready with another magic bubble. A line connected the bubble to the wizard's wand.

"Diego, now!" Drake yelled.

The bubble surrounded the baby dragon. He was out of energy, so he couldn't break the bubble this time.

Quick as a flash, Diego reached out and touched Worm. Worm glowed green.

Whoosh! Worm, Diego, and the quiet baby dragon transported to Diego's cottage.

"We did it!" Drake cheered.

Ana smiled at Carlos.

"I'm Ana, and this is Bo," she said. "You must be the new Dragon Master."

"I am — I mean, I think I am," Carlos said.

"You did a good job getting your dragon to calm down," Bo said. "We should take you to him right away."

Carlos shook his head. "I can't leave my abuela."

"Just come with us to Diego's cottage," Drake said. "It won't take long. Our dragons will fly us there."

"Well, okay," Carlos replied.

"Do you know how to get there?" Bo asked Drake.

Drake frowned. "No, I'm not sure where Diego's cottage is. We used magic to get here. And without Worm . . ."

Suddenly, he noticed a bird flying toward them. A white bird with a black head. Drake smiled.

"I might not know the way," he said. "But Bob does!"

CHAPTER 13

CARLOS DECIDES

Bob squawked.

"Come on, he wants us to follow him!" Drake said.

Drake climbed aboard Kepri, behind Ana. Carlos climbed aboard Shu, behind Bo. Then the dragons took off, following Bob.

Drake looked down. The fishermen had returned to the beach. They looked smaller and smaller as the dragons followed Bob along the coastline.

Soon, Drake spotted Diego's cottage. Bob swooped down and the dragons landed.

"Excellent!" Diego said, running over to them. "I'm glad Bob found you so quickly. And now the baby Lightning Dragon is safe inside the stable."

"Aren't you worried he'll shoot out sparks? Your cottage could catch on fire!" Ana said.

"Come and see," Diego said.

They all followed Diego to the stable. Worm was outside.

"I sent a magical message to Griffith," Diego said. "He and the others will be here soon."

Diego stopped and opened the top half of the stable door. The baby dragon was peacefully sleeping on the hay.

"Worm drained the baby dragon's energy back on the beach," Diego explained. "Griffith read that it will take several days for a Lightning Dragon to build up energy again. And in that time, Carlos, you can work on making your connection stronger."

"Come back to the castle and train with us!" Ana said.

Carlos shook his head. "I can't leave my abuela."

"You won't have to," Diego said.

Carlos's eyes got wide. "I won't?"

"No," Diego replied. "Griffith and I decided that the Lightning Dragon can stay here for now. You will stay with me. And we can visit your abuela every day."

"Really?" Carlos asked.

Diego nodded. "Really."

Carlos moved closer to the stable door. "He is a beautiful dragon."

"You should name him!" Ana said.

"Yes, that is a great idea," agreed Bo.

Carlos looked thoughtful. "How about Lalo?"

The Lightning Dragon opened his eyes and raised his head. He looked at Carlos. Carlos's Dragon Stone glowed faintly.

"He's not saying words, exactly," Carlos said. "But I am getting a feeling. A happy feeling."

"He will learn words, in time," Diego said. "He is just a baby, after all."

Drake looked at Ana and Bo. They all smiled. The Lightning Dragon was safe! And a new Dragon Master had joined them.

Clink! Clink!

The strings of seashells on the stable walls began to rattle. The walls of the stable began to shake.

Diego took out his wand.

"Danger is coming!" he yelled.

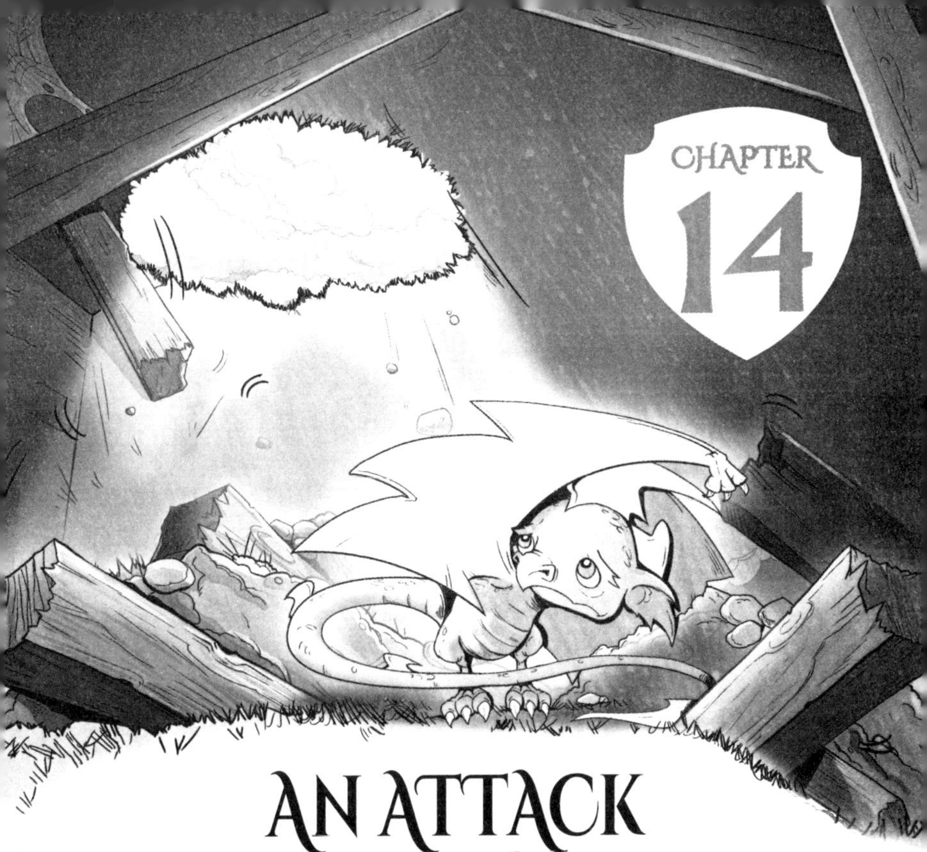

AN ATTACK FROM THE SKY

Boom! Boom! Boom!

The sound of thunder filled the air. Storm clouds quickly filled the sky. The roof of the stable split open. Wood and straw tumbled down on the Lightning Dragon.

Eeeeeeeeeee! The baby dragon cried out in confusion.

"Lalo!" Carlos yelled, pulling open the stable door.

A dragon dropped through the open roof. Drake gasped. The dragon had a long body, like Worm. But this dragon had four legs. Long whiskers flowed from its snout. Dark purple scales shimmered all over its body.

A black-haired woman was riding the dragon. A piece of the Dragon Stone glowed on a chain around her neck.

"Look! She's a Dragon Master!" Drake cried.

"And that — that is a Thunder Dragon!" Diego yelled. He raised his wand. "Be gone!" A blue energy bolt streamed from the wand toward the woman and her dragon.

She held out her hand, and a whip of purple light snaked out. It swept away Diego's blue energy bolt. Then her light snaked around the baby Lightning Dragon's neck.

"She's trying to steal Lalo!" Drake realized.

"Leave my dragon alone!" Carlos yelled at the woman.

"We have to stop her!" Ana cried, jumping on top of Kepri.

"Shu, water blast!" Bo commanded his dragon.

Shu aimed a powerful spray of water at the Thunder Dragon. But before the water hit, the dragon glowed with purple energy. The water bounced off.

The Thunder Dragon began to float upward.

"Worm, stop her!" Drake yelled.

Worm started to glow bright green. The Thunder Dragon froze. Drake knew that Worm was holding the dragon in place with his mind powers.

Then Drake's Dragon Stone lit up. He heard Worm's voice in his head.

Too strong.

The Thunder Dragon broke away from Worm's pull. It zoomed up and out of the stable, carrying the baby dragon.

"Lalo!" Carlos cried. His Dragon Stone was glowing. "I can feel how scared he is. We've got to help him!"

Ana, riding on Kepri, raced after them. The others ran outside to watch.

Suddenly, a hole opened up in the sky! It was made of purple, swirling energy.

A big wind blew down, throwing Kepri and Ana back to the ground.

The Thunder Dragon and its rider flew into the hole. They disappeared, taking Lalo with them.

CHAPTER 15

WE WON'T GIVE UP!

The hole in the sky closed up.

"Look!" Bo cried, pointing above the cottage.

Two dragons swooped down from the sky. Petra rode on the four-headed hydra, Zera. Rori and Griffith rode on Vulcan.

Zera and Vulcan landed beside Diego.

"What happened here?" Griffith asked. "We saw the sky open up in front of us!"

"We were attacked," Diego replied.

"Yes!" Drake said. "By a woman riding a Thunder Dragon. She stole Lalo – the baby Lightning Dragon!"

"And then she disappeared through a hole in the sky," Ana added.

Griffith's face darkened. "Eko," he said.

Diego nodded. "Yes, I believe that it was her."

"Who is Eko?" Rori asked.

Griffith didn't answer. He gazed up into the sky. Drake had never seen him look so worried.

"We need to rescue Lalo!" Carlos said.

"And we will help you, friend," Bo said.

"Of course we will," said Petra. "We won't let anything bad happen to your dragon."

"Eko had better not try to take Vulcan!" Rori said, making a fist.

Ana put her hand on Carlos's shoulder. "Don't worry," she said. "We will find Lalo."

"That's right!" said Drake. "We'll get him back, because we are Dragon Masters!"

TRACEY WEST visits the beaches of New Jersey every summer, where she likes watching the seagulls scurry across the sand. She talks to them sometimes, but so far, none of them have talked back!

Tracey has written dozens of books for kids. She does her writing in the house she shares with her husband and three stepkids. She also has plenty of animal friends to keep her company. She has three dogs, seven chickens, and one cat, who sits on her desk when she writes! Thankfully, the cat does not weigh as much as a dragon.

DAMIEN JONES lives with his wife and son in Cornwall – the home of the legend of King Arthur. Cornwall even has its very own castle! On clear days you can see for miles from the top of the castle, making it the perfect lookout for dragons.

Damien has illustrated children's books. He has also animated films and television programs. He works in a studio surrounded by figures of mystical characters that keep an eye on him as he draws.

DRAGON MASTERS

SEARCH FOR THE LIGHTNING DRAGON

Questions and Activities

How does each team take part in finding the Lightning Dragon?

Why does Diego have shells in every room of his cottage?

What does Carlos think of Drake and Diego when he first meets them?

Why is it important to drain the Lightning Dragon's energy?

Use pictures and words to retell the events that take place once the Thunder Dragon and Eko arrive at Diego's cottage.